The Owls of Blossom Wood

First published in the UK in 2016 by Scholastic Children's Books

An imprint of Scholastic Ltd
Euston House, 24 Eversholt Street
London, NW1 1DB, UK
Registered office: Westfield Road, Southam, Warwickshire, CV47 0RA
SCHOLASTIC and associated logos are trademarks and/or registered
trademarks of Scholastic Inc.

ISBN 978 1407 15667 5

A CIP catalogue record for this book is available from the British Library

Printed and bound by CPI Group (UK) Ltd, Croydon, CR0 4YY
Papers used by Scholastic Children's Books are made from wood
grown in sustainable forests.

5 7 9 10 8 6 4

www.scholastic.co.uk

The Owls of Blossom Wood

Save the Day

Catherine Coe

SCHOLASTIC

For Madeleine Cropley,
with lots of love xxx

With many thanks to the amazing team at the

Fritton Owl Sanctuary for your invaluable support –

and to your wonderful, inspirational owls.

Chapter 1
A Helpful Hoot

"When they're on land, loons are some of the clumsiest birds around," said the deep voice coming from the TV.

Katie laughed. "They sound a lot like you, Eva!"

"Hey!" Eva complained, though her green eyes were sparkling. "I'm not clumsy *all* the time!"

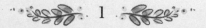

"But in the air and water, loons are fantastic flyers and swimmers," the voiceover continued.

"Well, we can't be good at everything," said Alex, putting an arm around Eva. The three girls were sitting next to each other on Alex's bed as they watched TV. "You might fall over a lot, but you make the BEST jewellery." Alex held up her bead bracelet — earlier, Eva had given Alex and Katie the home-made jewellery as presents. Alex's was purple, Katie's was pink, and Eva had one that was silver.

"You're right — our bracelets are beautiful!" Katie turned to Eva, biting her lip. "Sorry — I was only joking."

Eva grinned and nudged Katie gently. "I know!"

The girls turned their eyes back to the TV on the chest of drawers in Alex's

 2

bedroom. They lived next door to each other, and often had sleepovers like this. Really, they should have been asleep already, but Alex had insisted on watching just one more episode. She was addicted to nature!

"Loon feathers are so thick that they feel like fur – and these help them to swim well."

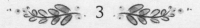

Katie grabbed the arms of her two friends. "The feather! Should we go and check for it?" She jumped up from the bed. "I think we should — just in case!"

The three best friends had a very special secret. Sometimes a glossy white feather was left out for them in a hollow tree trunk in Katie's garden. If it was there, they could take hold of it and travel to the magical Blossom Wood. Even more amazing was the fact that, whenever they were there, they weren't girls, but owls!

"But we looked in the tree trunk just before we cleaned our teeth." From the bed, Alex craned her neck towards her friend. Katie was standing up and tying back her long blonde hair as if she meant business.

"But that was ages ago — maybe it will be there now!"

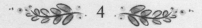

Eva shuffled out from under the duvet. "I think we should go and check just in case. We haven't been to Blossom Wood for over two weeks!"

Two weeks IS ages, thought Alex, leaping up too. For a second she worried about getting in trouble for going outside so late – but they were only going over to

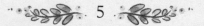

Katie's garden next door. She wrapped her turquoise dressing gown around her pyjamas, and pulled the hood over her black curly hair to keep her extra warm.

Once they were all huddled into their dressing gowns and fluffy slippers, they padded out of Alex's bedroom silently. Alex lived with her parents in a bungalow, so they could dart out of her bedroom and slip along the central hallway to the back door without any stairs to worry about. They could hear twangs of music floating out of the living room – Alex's dad played the guitar, and it sounded as if her mum was singing along to an old jazz tune.

Alex, Eva and Katie tiptoed down the garden path, the frosty air biting at their hands. Just past Alex's vegetable patch, Katie skipped towards the wooden fence. There was a gap here, where last week

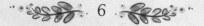

her brother had crashed his go-kart and broken a panel. Her mum had been furious, but Katie was pleased – it meant they could go easily between their next-door gardens. Perfect for tonight.

She bent down and squeezed through, emerging beside the end of the washing line. Eva went next, holding back her bobbed auburn hair so it didn't get

caught. Alex followed, not needing to crouch as much since she was the shortest of the friends.

"It's freezing!" said Eva, hopping over to the path to get away from the frosty grass. The girls could talk here without worrying they'd be heard, because Katie's parents were away for the night, and her brother was staying at their grandad's.

"Come on," called Katie, who was already sprinting towards the fallen tree trunk at the bottom of the garden.

But when Eva and Alex had caught Katie up, she was kneeling next to the trunk and shaking her head. "There's nothing there!"

Eva sighed deeply. "Oh, I really thought it might be. I've missed Blossom Wood so much!"

Alex thought of all their friends there – Bobby the badger, Loulou the squirrel,

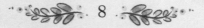

Winnie the wren – she missed them too. But at least no feather meant that there weren't any problems in the wood. Bobby only left the feather out if he needed their help.

Katie stood up and the girls began trudging back towards the broken fence, arm in arm. But Alex heard a noise that made her stop. The unmistakable hoot

of a barn owl. Did it mean anything? She shrugged – of course not, it was just nature. She skipped to catch up with Eva and Katie and heard it again. Louder this time.

"Wait a minute!" Alex called to her friends. She ran back down Katie's garden, not caring that her slippers were getting wetter and wetter from the frosty grass.

"What are you doing?" asked Katie, her blue eyes wide as she watched her friend zoom down the garden path.

"It's here!" cried Alex, feeling her heart racing faster than one of the loons from the documentary. Inside the trunk, the white feather glowed in the gloom.

Katie sped down the garden while Eva, already on the other side of the fence, leapt back through the gap. She tumbled right into the washing-line pole. "Oops!"

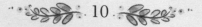

she said as she dusted herself down.

Moments later, all three girls were crouched inside the hollow chestnut tree trunk, with Alex clasping the feather super-tight. Just yesterday she'd been worrying that they'd never get to go back to Blossom Wood ever again. She wasn't going to let go of this feather for anything!

With her free hand, Alex grabbed Katie's, and Katie took Eva's. They squeezed their eyes shut, and waited...

The spinning began — slowly at first, as if they were on a carousel meant for toddlers, and then faster, as if they were on a merry-go-round. Soon it was going so quickly it felt like the craziest ride at a theme park. Eva's stomach swirled and she couldn't help but let out a squeal — she always felt like they were being thrown around inside a hamster ball. There was

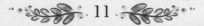

great whooshing too, as wind whistled past their ears. They were buffeted this way and that, but they never let go of each other's hands, nor opened their eyes. They didn't dare!

Katie whooped in delight as she felt

her toes tingling – a sign that they were very nearly there. *But what will be waiting in Blossom Wood for us this time?* she wondered. Why did the animals need their help? She hoped it wasn't anything too serious...

Chapter 2
All Abuzz

Eva opened her eyes slowly and took
in the amazing sight of Blossom Wood,
spread out in front of her as far as she
could see. She gazed at the bright green
trees of Apple Orchard, the sparkling
Willow Lake and the peaks of Echo
Mountains in the distance. She heard the
gentle sounds of the Rushing River, the

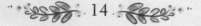

tweets of starlings and sparrows, and the tiny buzzing of insects.

The girls had arrived on one of the highest branches of the Moon Chestnut tree — although, just like every other time they came to Blossom Wood, they weren't girls any more. They were owls! Katie, a snowy owl, hopped along the branch, turning to her friends. She looked at Eva, now a barn owl with a soft white body and light brown wings. Then she took in Alex, who was a fluffy brown little owl and the smallest of the three.

"I'm so happy to be here again!" twittered Alex. She flapped up into the

air, enjoying the warm breeze in her feathers. It felt amazing to be able to fly again, and she zoomed up above the treetops.

Still on the branch, Katie wiped her forehead with a wing. "Wow, it's hot here today!"

"And it's busy, too!" Eva jumped back as a swarm of bees soared past her, buzzing furiously. She watched as more and more rushed through the trees, forming one giant, buzzing cloud.

A frown crept across Alex's round, feathery face. "What's wrong with the bees? They seem angry..." Usually, the bees would be buzzing about individually, happily flying between flowers and trees and plants to pollinate them. She'd never seen them in one enormous black buzz before. They filled the blue sky above

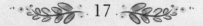

them like a storm cloud.

Eva held up a wing to shadow her eyes from the sun and looked at them closely. Her incredible owl eyesight meant she could see much further than when she was a girl. She squinted, noticing that lots of the bees were carrying something in their arms. "What are they holding?" she asked no one in particular.

Katie answered by leaping off the branch. "I don't know, but I'm going to find out!" She spread her white wings, flecked with black, and flew elegantly upwards. Katie's wings were so big she didn't have to flutter them much – and she felt like a gliding kite as she tilted about smoothly, this way and that.

The buzzing only worsened as she came closer to the bees. "They're holding signs!" she yelled back to Alex and Eva,

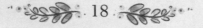

who had followed her. Even though her friends were now right behind Katie, she had to shout to make herself heard over the din.

The sound was worse than a hundred lawnmowers, thought Alex. She knew that something must have upset the bees greatly for them to be making such a fuss. Then she caught sight of what they were holding. Little tiny signs, with bee handwriting scrawled across them. "Bee Kind to Bees!" she read aloud.

"Better Bee Sorry!" Eva read another.

"Bees on Strike," twittered Katie.

The owls turned to each other at once. "The bees are on strike?!" hooted Eva.

"Oh no..." Katie put a wing to her beak.

"This is a disaster!" said Alex. Being on strike meant that the bees were refusing to do any work. It didn't just

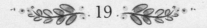

mean there would be no honey, it meant
the flowers and plants and trees weren't
being pollinated, which meant that fruit
wouldn't grow for much longer. It could
be terrible news for Blossom Wood!

She beckoned her friends back down to
the Moon Chestnut tree. They flew past
the curved trunk, towards the forest floor.
The tree was named after the fact that the
trunk was shaped like a crescent moon.

What's more, as it was the tallest and oldest tree in the whole of Blossom Wood, the woodlanders believed it was magical.

As Eva landed on the warm, dry soil, she caught sight of Bobby lumbering along a rough grass path. The badger huffed and puffed as he came closer. "You arrived quickly!" he gasped, in his deep, gravelly voice.

Alex smiled. "We came right away."

"And we saw the problem!" added Katie. "But why are the bees on strike?"

Bobby shrugged his shoulders and hung his stripy head sadly. "I wish I knew. It's been going on for a couple of days. I didn't want to bother you at first. I thought they'd give up and calm down. But today they look angrier than ever!"

"Oh, you're here!" squeaked a familiar voice. Eva turned to see Loulou

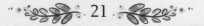

shimmying down the tree. The squirrel darted up to them, a nut in her paws. She began to nibble the edges quickly, as if she were eating corn on the cob, Alex thought.

"Do you know what's up with the bees?" Katie asked Loulou.

She stopped mid-bite. "I tried to ask, but they won't speak to me!" Loulou flicked her tail about, swallowed the rest of her nut and darted along the forest

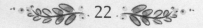

floor. "Got to go," she squeaked over her furry shoulder. "I'm in the middle of making a nutty nut sundae. Good luck with the bees!"

Bobby watched her go. "Many of the woodlanders don't realize how awful this is," he told Alex, Katie and Eva, his black eyes looking very serious. "But if the bees stop working, then soon many things in the wood will stop growing. I don't know what to do!"

"That's what I've been worrying about," said Alex. The little owl bobbed her fluffy head as if she had decided something. "Let me try to speak to the bees on my own. Maybe they'll talk to just one of us." Before her friends could stop her, she flapped her small wings, hopped once, twice, three times, and took off into the summer air.

Even though Alex was normally shy, she felt determined today, and there was one bee in particular she was hoping to talk to. Bella was just as timid as her, but Alex had spoken to her enough times to think of her as a friend. She wondered if she could manage to get her attention.

The buzzing swarm of bees seemed even bigger as Alex flew up to it by herself. She searched the black-and-yellow bodies for Bella, although the flickering insects made her feel a bit dizzy, especially as she still had to keep flapping her wings at the same time.

Just as her eyes were scanning the far tip of the bee cloud, Alex spotted her friend. "Bella!" she called. "Bella!"

The tiny bee's eyes widened at the sound of her name, and she buzzed forward, closer to Alex.

"Bella, what's happening?" Alex yelled to make herself heard over the buzzing of bees, which was tricky since she only had a little voice. "Why are you all on strike?"

Bella darted forward further. "Oh, I'm so glad you came. You see..." But before she could finish what she was saying, a group of bees surrounded Bella, buzzing and shaking their heads.

"Stop interfering!" shouted one who held a sign that read, "Buzz Off!"

Before Alex could reply, the whole swarm crowded even more tightly together, and flew towards their hive in the Moon Chestnut tree.

Alex watched them go, her beak gaping open in horror. Now what were they going to do?

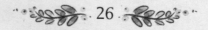

Chapter 3
Tea Time

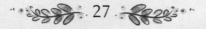

Alex flew back to her friends on the ground quickly, a worried frown across her fluffy face. She told them what had happened. "I'm sorry," she finished. "Not even Bella would talk to me."

"It's not your fault," said Bobby, putting a black paw on Alex's wing. "I don't know what's got into the bees, I truly don't."

"But *someone* in Blossom Wood must know what's wrong?" twittered Katie. She couldn't help but feel a bit impatient – what was so bad that it meant the bees wouldn't even talk to them?

"We could ask Winnie?" Eva suggested. "She always seems to know what's going on in the wood."

Bobby nodded. "Winnie would be an excellent creature to ask. Good luck, owls," he said, waving as the three friends flew up to Winnie's nest at the middle of the Moon Chestnut tree.

As soon as they arrived on the thick branch, Winnie fluttered out of the nest and smiled. It was a beautiful home, made of thick moss and shiny chestnut leaves. Above it towered a lily-pad umbrella – keeping the wrens shaded from the sun.

"Hello, Winnie!" called Katie. "Do you

know what's the matter with the bees?"

Winnie shook her head, making her tiny feathers bounce about. "I'm so very-berry sorry, but I have not one diddly-squat of an idea!" She turned back into the nest. "Do you know anything, kids?"

Below her, six little bird heads popped up all of a sudden, twittering madly. But they shrugged, their eyes wide. Not one

of Winnie's children knew what was wrong either.

Katie, Alex and Eva thanked Winnie, and promised they'd come to the wrens' choir practice tomorrow, if they were still in Blossom Wood. They left the branch of the Moon Chestnut tree and zoomed towards the ground. As she flew, Eva spotted the little green figure of Wilf the caterpillar, slithering from leaf to leaf.

"Wilf," she hooted, fluttering ahead of her friends to reach him. "Wait a minute!" For a caterpillar, Wilf was surprisingly quick, and Eva almost lost sight of him before he finally heard her shouts and twisted his tiny head. She held out a wing and he slithered on to it, grinning.

"Hi, Eva! Oh, it's great to see you! We haven't chatted in AGES! Would you like to come and see my latest silk creations?

Or can I interest you in some green-leaf soup? I made it myself!"

Eva smiled — she'd forgotten just how talkative the little caterpillar was. And he certainly didn't seem to realize there was any kind of problem in the wood. When she finally managed to get a word in edgeways, she asked, "Do you know

anything about the bees, and why they're refusing to do their usual work?"

Wilf shook his whole body from left to right. "Oh no, oh dear... No, I don't know anything about that. Perhaps they're fed up with making honey?"

But Eva didn't think it was that – the bees had told her they LOVED making honey. There had to be another reason. She thanked Wilf, told him she hoped to be able to join him for green-leaf soup another day (although, if she was honest, it didn't sound all that nice) and found Katie and Alex on the ground.

"Wilf didn't know anything either!" she told her friends. "What next?"

"We'll just have to keep asking!" said Katie, putting a wing over her mouth as she yawned. She wondered why she felt tired, and then realized – they had been

about to go to sleep when they came to
Blossom Wood. It might be daytime here,
but back home they should have been
tucked up in bed! But she couldn't think
about that — not when they had such an
important problem to solve.

They heard a rustling, and turned to
look at the sound. The familiar black-and-
white stripes of Bobby's head emerged
from a nearby blueberry bush.

He spotted the owls and plodded over
as fast as he could, not even stopping
to eat a berry, despite them being his
favourite.

"How did you get on?" he asked, his
worried voice sounding much higher than
usual.

Alex saw his mouth turn down, and
guessed he knew the answer just by
looking at their faces. She opened her

beak to reply, and a yawn popped out before she could stop it!

"Oh dear, you do all look awfully tired." Bobby's black eyes filled with concern. "Why don't you come back to mine for a quick refreshing cup of peppermint tea?"

Fighting to control her drooping eyelids, Katie thought that sounded like

the best idea she'd ever heard. "Yes, please, Bobby."

Eva nodded, thinking that sounded a lot tastier than green-leaf soup!

"Thanks, Bobby." Alex bobbed her head in agreement. "I think we all need it!"

The friends squeezed into Bobby's burrow. For Alex, the smallest of the owls, it was easy to hop into the little hole in the ground and through the mud-walled tunnel. For Eva, it was tricky, but if she ducked her heart-shaped head down, she could shuffle along. Katie found it much harder, and had to tuck in her wings tightly and bend halfway down to get inside!

Fortunately, once they made it into Bobby's pretty living room, lit by tea lights, there was much more space to spread about.

"Make yourselves comfortable," Bobby said, pointing a paw at the woven-grass rugs.

The friends smiled and sank bank into the soft material. It was lovely and cool in here, compared to the hot summer's day outside. *It's funny how the weather is always so different here compared to home*, thought Alex, remembering the freezing-cold weather they'd left behind.

Bobby passed them flower-shaped clay bowls filled with peppermint tea, and they pecked at it thirstily.

Katie felt her eyes un-droop immediately. She looked down at the tea. Was it magical?

"You must be hungry too, with all that rushing about you've been doing, trying to find out what's wrong with the bees." Bobby held out a wicker basket. "Here —

please have some of these honey-coated blueberries."

In answer, Eva's stomach rumbled like a train. She reached out and popped a berry into her mouth, remembering these were Bobby's favourite. She thought he was so

kind to share them. "Thanks, Bobby —
they're delicious!"

"The bees gave them to me just last
week," Bobby said with sad eyes. "They
had made them especially. Now they
won't even talk to me!"

"So they weren't on strike then?" Alex
drained the last of her tea, feeling much
more refreshed now.

Bobby shook his head. "No, no — they
seemed as happy as treetops!"

"I wonder what changed..." Katie
thought out loud.

"Has anything been different in the
wood?" Eva pressed.

Bobby put a paw to his chin, deep in
thought. "Well, the only thing I can think
of is that the ducks are back. They've just
recently returned to Willow Lake after the
winter. But I can't see why that would

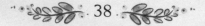

make the bees angry."

Alex couldn't think why either. She'd never heard of bees not getting on with ducks.

"Maybe it'd be worth us talking to the ducks just in case," twittered Katie.

"You're right!" Eva bounced up, feeling full of energy again, and forgetting she was in Bobby's burrow. She bashed her head on the ceiling. "Ouch!"

Bobby hurried over to check she was OK, but Eva grinned and waved a wing at him. "I'm fine, please don't worry – I'm used to bumping into things!"

Bobby followed the owls out of his burrow to wave them goodbye. He shielded his eyes from the hot midday sun, watching them take off into the deep blue sky.

"Oh, thank treetops you're here,

wonderful owls. I don't know what
Blossom Wood would do without you!"

Chapter 4
Quack, Quack!

As they flew away from Bobby's sett, Alex looked down and saw the badger shuffle over to the nearby waterfall and cup his paws to splash himself with the cool water. *He must be boiling today*, she thought, *with all that black fur. Although he's still wearing his scarf!* Alex, Katie and Eva rose higher, feeling the warm air under their outstretched wings, and soon Bobby became just a tiny dot beneath them.

In the distance, Willow Lake shimmered in the heat of the day, and they zoomed towards it. As the friends passed the tall top of the Moon Chestnut tree, they could hear the bees in their hive still buzzing like crazy. It reminded Katie just how important it was to find out what was bothering them and somehow make it better. She flapped her great wings even harder, determined to speak to the ducks as soon as she could.

As soon as they began their descent towards the lake, they spotted the ducks on the far side, amongst a thick patch of reeds. Or rather, they *heard* the ducks, and spotted them afterwards – their quacking was non-stop. It was almost as loud as the buzzing of the bees.

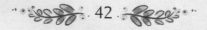 42

"Hello?" Katie asked tentatively, as they came down to land in the shade of a willow tree next to the reeds. It was cooler here, and Katie felt glad of it — she was hotter now than after a two-hour tap-dancing lesson!

"Quack, quack, quack," said a brown female duck. Alex could tell she was a

girl because she knew that female mallard ducks were brown, whereas the males had green heads and white, glossy bodies.

"Quack, quack," added another female beside her, who had pretty purple side patches below her wings. She'd been busy plaiting reeds to make a circular wall – or at least that's what it looked like to Eva. She guessed they were making a proper home for themselves now that they were back in Blossom Wood. It looked really cute!

Alex began to panic that the ducks couldn't say anything but *quack*. But at that moment, a male with a shiny green head and a bright yellow bill waddled forward, beaming.

"Hello, owls. We've heard lots about you." He put out a glistening wing. "I'm Montgomery Karbensten the Third. But that's such a mouthful, I know. We ducks

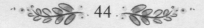 44

all have very long names. I can never remember them all... Anyway, please just call me Monty!"

He winked cheekily at them and then pointed at the female making the reed wall. "And this is my wife, Hampton Belvedere the Seventh."

His wife smiled and waved. "Please, call me Hampty!"

Eva shook Monty's wing and grinned. *These ducks look like fun*, she thought. "I'm Eva. And this is Katie, and Alex."

Katie stepped forward. "Monty, can I ask you a question? We're trying to work out why the bees are on strike. Do you have any idea?"

Monty shook his green head, and Hampty looked confused. "Why would they strike?" she asked.

"We don't know," twittered Alex. "But we were hoping you might be able to help, since they've only been striking since you've been back."

"But us ducks and the bees get on marvellously!" Hampty flapped her wings, then frowned. She turned to Monty. "You did send them an invite to our Duck Dance this afternoon, didn't you?"

Monty nodded his head so fast it was

a blur. "Yes — I delivered their invitation myself!"

"The Duck Dance?" Katie asked, confused.

"It's to celebrate being back in Blossom Wood," Hampty explained. "You owls must come, of course! Although perhaps we should cancel it, if the bees are on strike..."

Monty put a wing on his wife's shoulder. "But the bees love dancing! In fact, I'd go as far as saying they're the best dancers in the whole of Blossom Wood."

Alex bobbed her head. It did seem odd that the bees wouldn't be excited about the dance. "Can we see the invitation?" she asked. Perhaps it would give them a clue. Or maybe they were barking — or rather, *hooting* — up the wrong tree...

"Of course!" quacked Hampty. She waddled off inside the reed-wall circle.

Meanwhile, some of the other ducks slid into the lake, careful to avoid the frogs and toads floating about the water on lily pads.

Hampty returned moments later, clutching a piece of silvery-leaf paper in

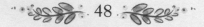

The ducks are back!

And we'd like to invite you to a special Duck Dance to celebrate!

This Friday afternoon, in Foxglove Glade.

Bring your dancing feet!

her bill. She held it out in front of the owls so they could read it:

The words were written in beautiful handwriting, in bright red ink. *It's the prettiest invitation I've ever seen!* thought Eva. She wondered if she might be able to take some of that paper back with her, to use for her invites for her birthday next month.

But Alex's beak had dropped open. Katie turned to her. "What's wrong?"

"It's red!" Alex replied.

Monty nodded, his eyes clouding with confusion. "We wrote them all in special red-berry ink. You don't like it?"

Alex shook her head. "Oh, it's not that – it looks very pretty – but the problem is, bees can't see the colour red!"

"Huh?" Katie and Eva hooted at the same time.

"It's true," Alex said, her head bobbing

even faster now. "It was on a documentary that we watched last week, remember?"

Katie couldn't quite remember it, but then they did watch at lot of nature programmes at Alex's, and Katie would sometimes half watch the TV and half practise her dancing in Alex's big bedroom at the same time. Alex had mirrored wardrobe doors, perfect for Katie to check her ballet poses!

Monty and Hampty both hung their heads. "Oh no!"

Hampty flapped her wings about in a panic. "Oh, quack! If they didn't get the invite – or at least, weren't able to read it – no wonder they're upset!"

Monty sucked in a deep breath. "What should we do, owls?"

"We can go and speak to the bees, and try to explain," Katie suggested.

"And in the meantime, can you write a new invitation in a different colour?" asked Alex.

"Consider it done!" quacked Hampty.

Chapter 5
Meeting the Queen

Katie, Eva and Alex fluttered outside the beehive nervously, not daring to get too close to the tremendous buzzing sound. "What in Blossom Wood are we going to say?" worried Alex. "They wouldn't listen to us before!"

"I think we should talk about the party," Katie decided, nodding her snowy-

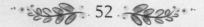

white head in determination. She flew even closer, and felt the vibrations from the buzzing ruffle her feathers as she drew near.

"Don't knock!" shouted Alex, as Katie raised a wing to do just that. Alex knew that tapping a beehive was the worst thing you could do — unless they wanted to make the bees even angrier, of course.

So Katie hovered in the air, her head almost touching the opening to the hive. She could smell sweet, delicious honey, and it made her mouth water. But now was not the time to think of her stomach!

"Hello, bees," said Katie, in the gentlest voice she could manage. "Are you on strike because you haven't been invited to the dance?"

The buzzing grew even louder then, like an orchestra of lawnmowers. It was as

if the bees were saying yes.

"But you *were* invited!" Katie explained.
The buzzing became even stronger, but
no one came close to the entrance – all
Katie could see was darkness.

Alex fluttered to Katie and put a wing
on her shoulder. "I think we need to
talk to the queen. She's the one who's in
charge." She put her beak close to
the opening. "Please may we speak with

Her Majesty, the Queen Bee?" As she spoke, Alex crossed her talons.

The bees went suddenly silent for a moment. Alex felt herself shaking with nerves. Perhaps it was extremely rude to ask to talk to the Queen Bee? She really didn't know what the rules were – all she knew was that in every hive, there was just one queen.

The buzzing started again, and Alex stared into the gloom of the hive. She realized that something was zooming slowly towards her: a big bee, at least double the size of the others, wearing a little silver crown. It had to be the queen! Her mouth was straight, her face stern.

Alex did a funny little curtsy in the air, but the Queen Bee's face didn't get any happier. "What do you want?" she buzz-barked in a scary, strict voice. "My

hive are all VERY upset that we have
not been invited to the dance. And after
everything we do for the wood and all
the animals who live here! We work SO
VERY HARD."

"But you were invited," Alex told her
quietly. "It's just that you couldn't read
the invitation – because it was written in
red..."

The bee frowned deeply. "What in

Blossom Wood are you talking about?"

Alex wasn't sure what to say. How could she explain this to the queen?

"Here!" Eva hooted from behind her.

Alex swivelled her head around. Her friend was holding out a red berry in her talon. Eva flew it closer to the Queen Bee.

"Can you see this?" Eva asked gently as she hovered in the air.

The Queen Bee reared up. "What? Are you playing a joke on us? There's nothing there!"

Eva scooped up the red berry on to a wing and carefully brought it right next to the Queen Bee. "There's a berry on my wing," she explained. "You can't see it because it's red, but it's there, I promise."

The bee stared at the wing, buzzing up and down it, frowning harder and harder.

Then she shot up suddenly as her wing brushed the berry. "What's that?!"

She dived down again to the same place, and the owls watched her lightly touching the little fruit with her wing, feeling all around it. "Oh, honey-crumbs! You're right! I can't see it ... but I can feel it!" She put her wings to her face and darted back inside the hive.

Katie, Alex and Eva could hear her buzzing to the bees inside. They hoped

she was explaining what had happened.

As they waited, a quack in the air above made them jump. Katie looked up, and spotted the brown figure of Hampty. She dived down towards them, and Katie noticed something in her beak – a new invitation for the bees! The best friends moved aside so that Hampty could deliver the invitation to the hive. As she dropped it in the little hole, the buzzing became crazy – but instead of an angry thunderstorm type of buzz, this sounded much more like cheering.

The Queen Bee poked her head back out. Her face was completely different now – smiley but also apologetic. "We are so very sorry – we really believed we weren't invited to the dance."

Hampty nodded as she flapped her large brown wings in front of the hive.

"*I'm* sorry we sent you an invitation you couldn't read, quack quack!"

"At least it's all sorted now," twittered Eva. The three best friends smiled at each other, feeling mightily relieved they'd solved the problem at last.

But then Alex noticed that the frown had returned to the Queen Bee's face. The creature was looking out past Hampty, Katie, Alex and Eva – towards the huge, beautiful Blossom Wood.

"What's wrong?" Alex asked.

The Queen Bee put a wing to her forehead. "We're so very behind on pollinating everything – there's so much to catch up on! Oh dear, oh dear...!"

"Can we help?" Eva offered. "If all the birds and flying insects in the wood joined in, hopefully it'd make a difference?"

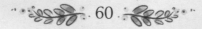

Alex clapped her wings together. "That's a great idea – I'd forgotten that it's not just bees who can pollinate things!"

"Oh, thank you, owls. You really are so helpful and kind!" The Queen Bee beamed and the three best friends performed a mid-air curtsy, as Alex had done earlier. She was royalty, after all!

The queen beckoned to the hundreds of bees in the hive, and they began zooming out – no longer angry but

determined to work hard.

Meanwhile, Hampty flew off and helped spread the word – asking anyone who could fly to help the bees. Katie, Eva and Alex did the same, approaching every bird, butterfly, dragonfly and firefly they saw to ask if they could move pollen from flower to flower, on plants, bushes and trees.

"This is fun, actually!" tweeted Katie as she hovered close to a honeysuckle plant, poked her beak into a flower and pecked up some sticky yellow pollen. She spun a pirouette in the air and shot over to another honeysuckle, dropping the pollen in one of its flowers.

Eva thought it looked like an amazing but complicated dancing display, with so many creatures flying this way and that. It reminded her of the maypole dancing they'd done at Bobby's birthday!

And she was realizing just how hard the bees had to work every day. It was exhausting!

Alex was heading towards a patch of poppies when she heard a small voice behind her. "Hi!"

She fluttered around and saw Bella shooting towards her, smiling from wing to wing. "We've finished – you can stop now! The Queen Bee says we're all caught up. We bees are flying around to tell everybody. Thanks so much, for everything. Without you, we'd still be on strike!"

Katie and Eva, working nearby, overheard Bella and came to join Alex. "That's brilliant!" Alex was saying to Bella, flapping her little wings in happiness.

The three owls and the bee headed downwards, landing on the mossy ground

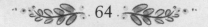

near the Moon Chestnut tree.

"I guess that means we should go home," twittered Eva, feeling a wave of sadness at leaving the magical wood behind once again. Katie's and Alex's wings drooped at the thought.

A frantic flapping sound made them jump. Monty appeared from behind the Moon Chestnut's trunk. "Excuse me, owls,

but I couldn't help but hear you. You can't go yet – you must come to our Duck Dance!"

"Oh, yes," buzzed Bella. "You have to stay for that! Please say you will?"

The three best friends swivelled their heads to one another, and slowly grinned great big smiles. They'd almost forgotten about it, but Bella was right – they couldn't miss their first Blossom Wood Duck Dance!

Chapter 6
Let's Dance!

Bright afternoon sunlight poured into
Foxglove Glade, lighting up the whole
area like a dance floor. Luckily the sun
wasn't quite as hot now, but it did make
the foxgloves around the glade glow
like disco lights. Not for the first time,
Eva wondered if magic was at work in
Blossom Wood.

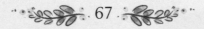

Creatures of all shapes and sizes were filling the glade, chattering and buzzing and squeaking and hooting. Eva waved at Wilf, and Winnie, and Mo and May, their mice friends. At one side, where the grass sloped up to form a stage, several of the ducks waddled about busily. When Eva looked closer, she realized they were all holding instruments of one kind or another — pine-cone drums, reed whistles and hazelnut cymbals. Hampty was carrying what looked like a trumpet made out of a red tulip, and Monty held a little wooden guitar under his wing!

Everyone stopped talking as one of the smaller ducks bashed the drums a few times, and Monty waddled to the front of the stage. "Thank you all for coming, woodlanders! We're so happy to be back in Blossom Wood. And we want to say

a special thanks to the wonderful owls, without whom this Duck Dance probably wouldn't have happened today!"

Hampty quacked loudly then, and Monty turned to her. She shuffled to the edge of the stage to join her husband. "And we mustn't forget the wonderful bees. Without you, nothing in Blossom

Wood would grow, and we really do appreciate you working so very hard every day. Thank you, thank you, thank you!"

A great round of applause echoed in the glade as the creatures clapped paws, pads, wings and hooves to thank the owls and the bees. Alex could feel her fluffy cheeks burning as everybody turned to look at them – she wasn't very good at being in the spotlight.

But the band started up quickly, so there wasn't much time to feel embarrassed. Before Alex knew it, she felt a wing in each of hers – Eva and Katie had grabbed her and begun twirling and dancing around. They kicked out their feet and swayed with their tail feathers, grinning from ear to ear as all the woodlanders joined in with the

dancing. Even Charles the blackbird, who was known for being rather grumpy, spun around with a smile. But then Eva noticed there was someone missing... Bobby was sitting at the edge of the glade, smiling and tapping a paw in time to the music. She hopped over and held out a wing.

"Come and dance, Bobby – it's so much fun!"

Bobby grinned but shook his stripy head. "Oh, I'm rather too old for all that. And truthfully, I can't dance for chestnuts! But I don't mind at all – I'm having a marvellous time just watching you all and trying the delicious dance drinks!"

Eva smiled back at Bobby as he raised an acorn cup filled with blueberry fizz. "OK, then – I'll come and say hello again

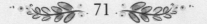

later!" She skipped across to the dance
floor, and found Bella facing Alex and
Katie, wiggling about in the air.

"Bella's teaching us the Honeybee
Waggle!" Katie explained as Alex and
Katie wiggled their feathery bottoms in
time to the music.

"Oh, that looks like fun." Eva hopped

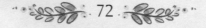

along beside them and began to copy
Bella too, wiggling one way, and then the
other, waving one wing to the right, then
one to the left.

It's a bit like doing the samba! thought
Katie, remembering a dance she'd learnt
at one of her classes.

Alex couldn't stop giggling as she jiggled
left and right — she'd never wiggled her
bottom about so much in her life!

As the song came to an end and the
next one started, more ducks joined
the duck band on the stage. "It's time
to perform our special Duck Jive!"
announced Monty with a wink. "Some
of you will know this one — and if you
don't, you can follow our duck dancers!"

The ducks lined up with their wings
in the air, and the band started playing a
quick, jumpy tune.

"This reminds me of the hokey-cokey!" Eva said to her friends as they kicked out their legs, one at a time, and then spun around, copying the ducks as best as they could.

After the Duck Jive, the worms and caterpillars cleared a space in the middle of the glade and did the Worm Dance – jumping down headfirst, then flipping up their bottoms again and again, slithering across the dance floor backwards. Everyone clapped and whooped, especially when Jonny the beaver and Loulou the squirrel joined in!

"I wish I could do that!" Katie hooted, her eyes wide.

"It might be possible as a girl," whispered Eva. "But I think as an owl it's probably impossible!"

"I'm going to try it as soon as we get

home!" Katie decided, unable to stop a yawn slipping out of her mouth as she spoke.

Alex put a wing on each of her friends. "Talking of home, maybe we should get back now? This has been brilliant — but I'm so tired I could fall asleep on my feet!"

Katie laughed. "Well, as owls, we can actually do that, remember! But you're right." Even though Katie hated to admit it, she felt shattered.

Eva nodded, feeling her eyelids droop at the talk of sleep. "It's been a VERY, VERY long day — but a brilliant one!"

They fluttered over to say goodbye to Bobby. The badger was busy chatting to Sara, one of the deer, as they watched the dancing and sipped at drinks from palm-leaf cups. "Oh my, you do look tired," Bobby said to the owls as they approached. He patted the ground next to

him. "Would you like to join us for
a rest?"

Alex shook her head sadly. "We should
get going. But we've had a fantastic time."

Bobby smiled. "I understand. Thank you

so much for helping the bees, and I'm
sorry it was so exhausting!"

"Oh, it was worth it!" Katie replied,
looking over to the dance floor, where
the bees had joined together into a long,
buzzing conga. Every single one of them
beamed as they zoomed around the edge
of the glade.

Eva waved as she, Alex and Katie began
fluttering into the bright blue afternoon
sky. "See you soon!"

But hopefully not too soon! thought Alex,
since they'd only be able to come back if
there was another problem in the wood

for them to help with.

"Thank you, owls!" Bobby watched them fly away before turning back towards the dancing once more.

The owls could hear the funky sounds of the duck band all the way to the top of the Moon Chestnut tree. They landed on the branch they'd arrived on, reached out to hold wingtips and grinned. "Goodbye, Blossom Wood," called Katie, as they closed their eyes and began to feel the familiar spinning and whooshing.

"Thanks for another amazing adventure!" added Eva, feeling her feathers ruffle in the wind.

Alex shut her eyes tighter and, although she didn't much like the spinning, she smiled. Blossom Wood was *always* amazing. She felt so lucky to be a part of it – and with her two best friends by her side!

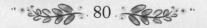

Did You Know?

❀ Bees pollinate by moving pollen grains from one flower to another. Moving the pollen like this means fruit can grow.

❀ If it's strong enough, the wind can also pollinate, by blowing pollen from one flower to another!

❀ Strangely, bees really can't see the colour red! They also really do perform a waggle dance!

❀ Honeybees make such a loud buzzing noise because they beat their wings two hundred times per second.

❀ Monty doesn't quack in the story because male mallard ducks don't quack – it's only the females that make this sound. Males make a quieter rasping noise.

Look out for more

The

Owls of

Blossom Wood

adventures!

The Owls of Blossom Wood

A Magical Beginning

Catherine Coe

The Owls of
Blossom Wood
❋ To the Rescue ❋

Catherine Coe

The Owls of Blossom Wood

Lost and Found

Catherine Coe

The Owls of Blossom Wood

The Birthday Party

Catherine Coe

The Owls of
Blossom Wood
An Enchanted Wedding

Catherine Coe

❀ Would you like more animal
fun and facts?

❀ Fancy flying across the treetops in
the Owls of Blossom Wood game?

❀ Want sneak peeks of other
books in the series?

Then check out the Owls of
Blossom Wood website at:

theowlsofblossomwood.com